LENORE'S

By SUSAN PEARSON

Illustrated by NANCY CARLSON

VIKING

VIKING
Published by the Penguin Group
Viking Penguin, a division of Penguin Books USA Inc.,
375 Hudson Street, New York, New York 10014, U.S.A.
Penguin Books Ltd, 27 Wrights Lane, London W8 5TZ, England
Penguin Books Australia Ltd, Ringwood, Victoria, Australia
Penguin Books Canada Ltd, 10 Alcorn Avenue, Toronto, Ontario, Canada M4V 3B2
Penguin Books (N.Z.) Ltd, 182–190 Wairau Road, Auckland 10, New Zealand
Penguin Books Ltd, Registered Offices: Harmondsworth, Middlesex, England

First published in 1992 by Viking Penguin, a division of Penguin Books USA Inc.

1 3 5 7 9 10 8 6 4 2

Library of Congress Cataloging-in-Publication Data
Pearson, Susan.
Lenore's big break / by Susan Pearson ;
illustrated by Nancy Carlson. p. cm.
Summary: A mild-mannered secretary changes her image and makes her dreams come true when she takes her talented birds on "Amateur Hour."
ISBN 0-670-83474-2 (hardcover)
[1. Birds—Fiction. 2. Secretaries—Fiction.]
I. Carlson, Nancy L., ill. II. Title.
PZ7.P323316Le 1992 [E]—dc20 91-29842 CIP AC

Printed in Mexico Set in 14 point Cushing Book

To Doris Smith, adventurous spirit,
"aunt" of distinction

—S.P.

Dedicated to Glen and Elaine—
who have watched my children and
hundreds of foster babies. Thanks!!!!

—N.C.

Everyone at the office thought Lenore was a nerd. They laughed at her clothes. They snickered at her broken nails. They made jokes about her hairstyle.

No one ever invited her to go along to the movies or out for dinner. "She's such a frump," they said. "We don't want to be seen with *her*."

Lenore ignored them. She had more important things to think about. Lenore had Big Plans.

I'd rather be shopping
TAMM I

Every day at five o'clock, she tidied her desk. She buttoned her baggy sweater and picked up her "Save the Iguanas" tote bag.

Before going home, she stopped at the Feed & Seed store for ten pounds of suet and five bags of sunflower seeds. She dropped into the bakery for fifteen loaves of day-old bread.

She rushed to the fish market for a few dozen cod.
She stopped by Barney's Bait Shop for some
buckets of worms and grasshoppers.

Then she climbed the unlit stairs
and unlocked her apartment door.

"Time to practice!" she called to her birds.

Everyone got right to work. The pelicans lined up
for their tap dance while the orchestra tuned up.

Meredith and Harvey climbed up onto the high wire.
George and Gracie ran through their vaudeville routine.

The jazz combo swung into "Stardust." Fred and Ginger waltzed around the dining room. Carmen and José worked on their tango.

Lenore led the hummingbirds through their aerobatics.
David did his magic act with the robins.

The flamingos performed *Swan Lake*.

They rehearsed until midnight. "We're getting better," Lenore told them, "but we still have a long way to go. Dinner now, and then bed. We'll practice more tomorrow night."

Night after night, Lenore and her birds rehearsed.

Day after day, she went to the office. Everyone thought she looked nerdier than ever. "She ought to do something with herself," they said. "Just look at those bags under her eyes."

Lenore paid no attention.

And then one night at dinner, Lenore announced, "We're ready!"
The birds all cheered. They sewed costumes until dawn.

In the morning Lenore quit her job. Everyone at the office thought she had flipped. "She'll never find another job," they said. "She must have lost her marbles."

Lenore just smiled.

She and her birds spent the whole day getting ready.

That night they appeared on "Amateur Hour."

They were the hit of the show. Calls flooded the station.

The next morning's paper carried the story:
LOCAL GIRL BIG HIT WITH BIRDS!
No one at the office knew what to say.

Lenore and her birds were an overnight success. The offers came pouring in. Lenore accepted only the best: a European tour, several shows in Las Vegas, Monte Carlo, and Palm Beach,

a Hollywood movie,

an after-school television special.

Everyone at the office followed her adventures with interest. They read about her in magazines. They heard about her on the radio. They stayed up late to catch her on television.

They taped her pictures up on their walls. “That Lenore,” they said. “We always knew she’d be a star.”

Lenore had always known it, too.

Pearson, Susan

Lenore's big break

DATE DUE

OCT 1 5 1993		Sherissa	5
Oct 18, 02		Andrea	

Silverton School Library
1160 Snowden
Box 128
Silverton, CO 81433